This book belongs to

High Hopes

Published by Advance Publishers
www.advance-publishers.com

Written by Ronald Kidd
Illustrated by Jeffrey Oh and Andrew Phillipson
Editorial development and management by Bumpy Slide Books
Illustrations produced by Disney Publishing Creative Development
Cover design by Deborah Boone

ISBN: 1-57973-026-4

It was early fall, and in the ravine next to Ant Island the last bunch of wildflowers was blooming.

Dot stood among the flowers one breezy
afternoon, enjoying the sunshine. She looked up at
Gypsy, who was flying from blossom to blossom.

Dot loved watching Gypsy the moth fly. Dot herself hoped to fly one day when her wings grew in. But she knew that was months away.

In the meantime, it seemed Dot had to settle for just watching.

Or did she?

As Dot sat there, a bright green moth fluttered by in the breeze. When it landed, Dot saw that it wasn't a moth at all. It was a leaf that had fallen from a tree. She looked up and saw more leaves falling.

In an instant, she had an idea.

Excited, Dot made her way to the base of the tree. She climbed up the trunk and along a limb, stepping out onto one of the leaves. There she stood, eagerly waiting for the leaf to fall.

Instead, another leaf fell, and another. Dot scrambled from leaf to leaf, trying to guess which would fall next. Somehow she never picked the right one.

14

Finally, exhausted, Dot lay down to rest on one of the leaves. As she slept, the breeze turned into a strong wind, rocking the leaf and waking her up.

"Yikes!" cried Dot. She held on, frightened, as the leaf swayed harder and harder. Suddenly the leaf broke off and went sailing through the air.

Dot was no longer frightened. "Wow!" she cried. "I'm really flying!"

Swooping down over Ant Island, she called to her friends, but they couldn't hear her.

Then, on the edge of the island, she saw Flik. He was trying to invent a machine to collect dewdrops.

"Hey, Flik!" shouted Dot. "Look up here! I'm flying!"

Flik looked at her and waved.

Just then another gust of wind caught the leaf, carrying Dot away. Worried, she called down, "Help me, Flik!"

"Hang on!" he shouted back. "I'll follow you!"
Flik got out his leaf telescope and watched where
the leaf took Dot. Then he quickly set out after her.

Dot, meanwhile, had landed in a spider web. It was the web built by her new friend Rosie, who had arrived with the other circus bugs.

Dot tried to wiggle free, but she realized she
was stuck in the web. "I guess I'll just have to wait
for Flik," she decided. "He'll be able to help."

The sunlight faded. Soon a long-legged creature came out of the grass and began climbing toward her. Dot couldn't tell what it was.

"Flik! Help!" she called out.

"I'm right here," said the creature. It was Flik! His long "legs" were twigs that he was holding with his hands and feet. That way, he could climb the web without getting stuck himself.

Flik helped Dot out of the web, and she thanked him for rescuing her.

"Oh, it wasn't hard, really," he said. "I just thought about the problem and tried to solve it using whatever was handy."

As they headed home, Dot told Flik about her adventure. "Did you ever fly?" she asked him.

"Sometimes I float on dandelion puffs," Flik told her.

"The funny thing is I always end up landing in strange places," Flik continued. "I'm never quite sure where the wind will take me. Maybe one day I'll invent the perfect flying machine."

Dot smiled up at Flik. Then she hurried home.

For the next few days, Flik didn't see her.

When Dot finally appeared, she ran up to him, saying, "Hey, Flik! Come with me—quick! I want to show you something!"

Dot led him up a tall tree, to a knothole. In the
knothole rested a leaf, weighted down by pebbles.
Flik studied the leaf. "Well, that's awfully nice, Dot,"
he said. "But, er, what exactly is it?"

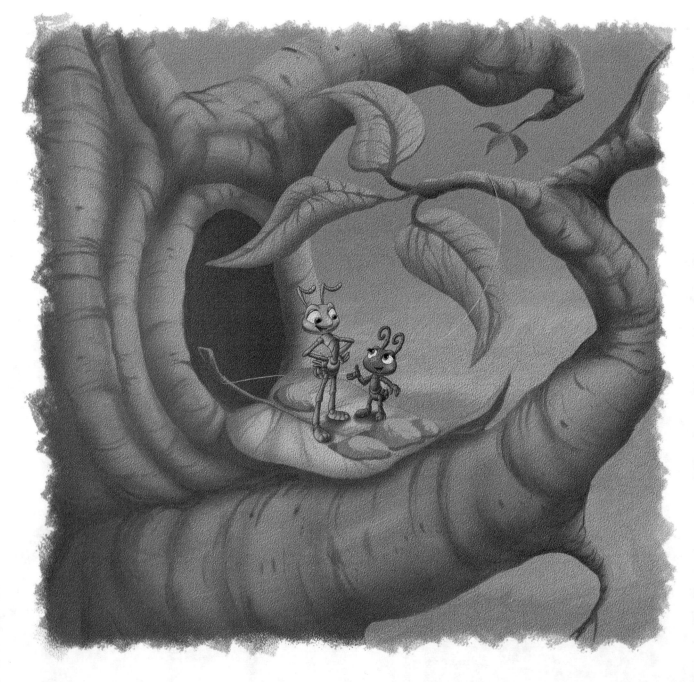

"Come on, and I'll show you," Dot said excitedly. Then she pushed away the pebbles. Free of extra weight, the leaf rustled in the breeze and lifted off, with Dot and Flik on it!

Flik was thrilled, but he was also nervous. "Gee, this is swell," he said. "But aren't you afraid we'll blow too far away?"

Dot grinned. "Nope. Just wait and see!" she told him.

The wind swirled, carrying them higher and higher. At last, when they reached the treetops, Dot looked down to the ground and gave a signal. There was a bump, and the leaf stopped rising.

"See?" said Dot. "I told you not to worry!"
Flik looked at her with admiration.

"How did you do that?" Flik asked.

"Simple," Dot said proudly. "This isn't just any old leaf. It's my first invention!"

Dot showed him a long, silvery thread that
was attached to the leaf and reached all the way
to the ground.

"Rosie made it for me," she told him.

Flik looked over the edge. Sure enough, on the ground far below were Rosie and Dim.

Dot explained, "Now I can fly like Gypsy, but I know that I won't blow too far away and get lost."

Flik beamed. Dot's first invention was one that even he would be proud of!

"Flik," asked Dot, "do you think I can be an inventor like you when I grow up?"

Flik smiled. "I think you already are an inventor!"
"Wow!" exclaimed Dot.

Then Dot gave a signal, and once again they began to move. Rising high above the treetops, the two friends gazed off across the countryside.

Far below was tiny Ant Island, where so many more adventures lay in store for them.

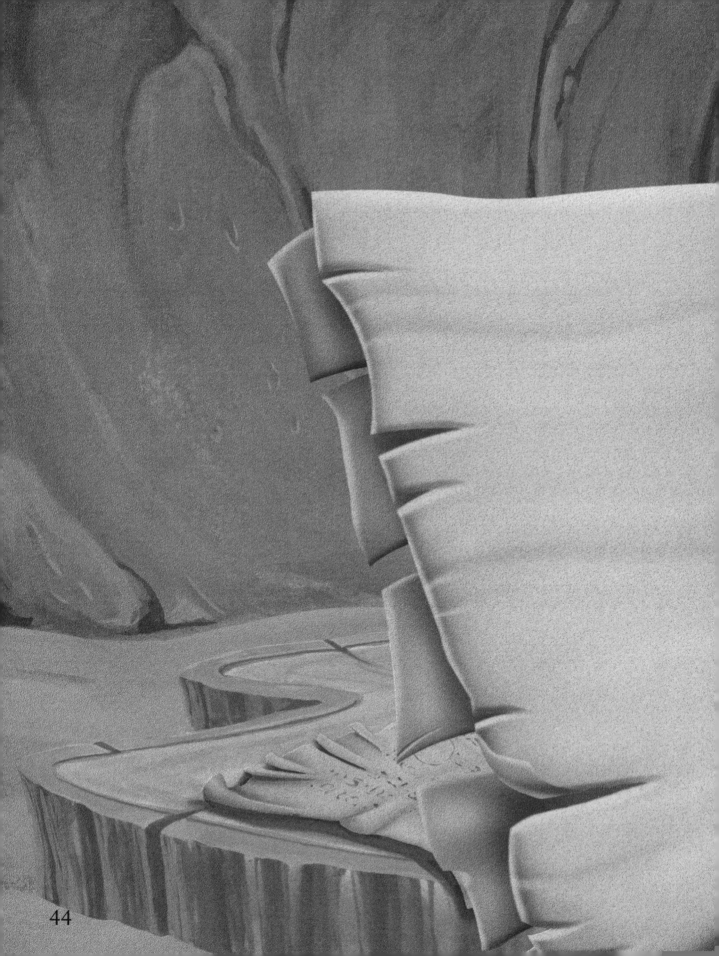

Dear Blueberry Journal,

Today Rosie told me about spider webs. I never knew there were so many kinds!

Different spiders make different kinds of webs. Some webs are in the shape of a wheel. Other webs are like tunnels. Others look like sheets, pieces of pie, or hammocks! There are even spider webs that are decorated with zigzags around the edges.

Rosie pulls the silky threads from her body to weave her web. The threads are very thin, but if they are twisted together they can be much stronger.

I'm glad they're strong, because I need them to keep my flying leaf from blowing away!

Till next time,
Dot